MEET ALL THESE FRIENDS IN BUZZ BOOKS:

The Animals of Farthing Wood
Thomas the Tank Engine
Biker Mice From Mars
Winnie-the-Pooh
Fireman Sam
Rupert
Babar

First published in Great Britain 1995 by Buzz Books,
an imprint of Reed Children's Books,
Michelin House, 81 Fulham Road, London SW3 6RB
and Auckland, Melbourne, Singapore and Toronto

ISBN 1 85591 458 1

Printed in Italy by Olivotto

To the Rescue

Story by Colin Dann
Text by Mary Risk
Illustrations by The County Studio

The Farthing Wood animals carried on, despite the threat of the rats who had infested White Deer Park.

Plucky, the grandson of the Farthing Wood Fox, was full of energy as usual.

"Let's race, Dash!" he said to the hare. "We'll practise first, then meet at the pond."

"Sssilly young fox," hissed Adder. "He'll never beat the hare."

Her mate, Sinuous, slithered alongside her and sniggered.

"At least I run faster than the rats," boasted Plucky. "I caught five last night."

Plucky sped off to the pond. There he found the two badgers drinking.

"Hello, Plucky," said Hurkle.

"Come join us," Shadow invited him.

As Plucky went to take a sip, a terrifying roar filled the air. Trey had arrived.

"Get away from my pond!" snarled the leader of the stags.

Shadow went on drinking as if she hadn't heard. With a snort of rage, Trey tossed her into the water with his antlers.

"Shadow!" called Hurkle in alarm.

Plucky could see that Hurkle was going to be next. He crept up behind the stag and bit his leg. Then he raced away, with Trey bellowing in hot pursuit.

Hurkle helped Shadow out of the water.

"I'm sure Trey is very kind, really," he said.

"You think everyone is kind," said Shadow.

A mound of earth suddenly appeared, and Mossy the mole popped out of it.

"Hello, Hurkle!" he said happily. "I've been looking for you!"

"And I'm looking for Plucky," said Dash, who had run up behind them. "Has he started the race without me?"

"Plucky is being chased by Trey," Shadow told him. "But Trey will never catch him."

Dash sat down to wait. She waited and waited, but Plucky didn't come.

"Something's wrong," she said at last.

11

Dash was searching the park for Plucky
when she came upon a pair of squirrels.

"Have you seen Plucky?" she asked them.

"No," said the squirrels. "Have you seen
our dad? He disappeared a few days ago."

Dash went to see Fox.

"Plucky's disappeared," she told him.
"And so have some of the other animals.
There's something odd happening here."

"Oh dear," said Fox. "We must find them."

Dash ran on, determined to find Plucky
and the other missing animals.

"Plucky!" she called. "Where are you?"

At the edge of White Deer Park, she stopped. Two men were in the car park, lifting cages into the back of a truck.

Something moved in a cage, then it squeaked. Dash's whiskers twitched.

"Squirrels!" she thought. "They're being kidnapped!"

14

Dash hopped nearer to the edge of the park, and tried to see into the van. It was full of cages! And in one cage, she could see a red furry body and a bushy tail.

It looked like a fox! It looked like Plucky!

15

The men shut the door to the back of the
van, then one of them jumped into the
front seat. The van began to move away.

"I must follow Plucky!" thought Dash.

The van went faster. Dash ran as she
had never run before. Her breath came in
panting gasps and her paws flew along
the ground.

At last, the van turned in through a pair
of high gates. Dash hopped up to the
gates, but they slammed in her face with
a clang.

"Poor Plucky," thought Dash. "He's a
prisoner. I've got to help him. But how?"

Sadly, she turned round and began to
hop back to White Deer Park.

As soon as his cage door opened, Plucky
darted out. He had to escape. The new
park was large, with plenty of room to
run, but Plucky wanted to go home.

He met one of the squirrels from White
Deer Park, who told him that he wanted
to go home, too. But neither Plucky nor
the squirrel could find a way out.

18

At White Deer Park, Dash ran straight
to see Fox and Vixen.

"Plucky's been kidnapped!" she told
them. "We've got to rescue him. Come
with me. I'll show you the car park
where I saw the truck."

Fox rose stiffly to his aging feet.

"Let's go, Dash," he said. "We've got to
rescue Plucky.

Fox was too old to run fast. He plodded after Dash until finally they reached the car park.

"There's the van!" shouted Dash.

Fox watched carefully as a man loaded a cage into the back of the van.

"That's the warden," he said. "He wouldn't hurt us. We can trust him."

"Why did he take Plucky?" asked Dash.

"I don't know, Dash, but we'll find out," said Fox, sounding more like his clever old self. "We need someone to go to this prison place and tell us what's inside."

Fox called a meeting of all the animals.

"The warden has taken some of our friends to a place with very high walls," Fox told them.

Everyone looked frightened.

"Now, I'm sure we can trust the warden," said Fox," but we want the animals back."

Fox turned to the heron. "Whistler, I
want you to fly over the high walls and
find our friends."

Whistler rose into the air.

"Good luck, matey!" croaked Toad.

From above, Whistler saw a truck pull
out of the car park. He followed it to the
gates, where the truck turned in. Whistler
soared over the gates and crash-landed
beak-over-tail inside the high walls.

Plucky ran up to him.

"Plucky, it's good to see you," gasped Whistler. "Are you all right?"

"Oh, yes," said Plucky. "This is a new animal sanctuary. It's great, but I miss my friends, especially Dash."

"And we miss you," said Whistler. "We need you. The rats are getting worse."

"But there's no way out," said Plucky.

The sound of an engine gave Whistler an idea. "Look, that truck is leaving. Hop on and it will take you through the gates. Hurry, Plucky!"

Plucky bounded up to the truck and jumped into the back. The squirrel was close behind. The gates shut behind them.

The truck driver drove quickly. Plucky shut his eyes. The speed made him feel dizzy. At last the truck slowed down.

"Jump!" Whistler called. "I'll show you the way home."

Plucky and the squirrel leapt to the ground, then followed the great heron home to White Deer Park.

At White Deer Park, Plucky saw Hurkle
and Mossy in a clearing. Then Dash
hopped past.

She stopped and looked at Plucky in
amazement. Gently, she touched him on
the nose with her paw.

"Plucky, it's you," she whispered. "It's really you!"

"It's me all right," said Plucky, smiling.

It was good to be home.